Unspoken Words

Sapiosexual
Demisexual
Are the things that drive me
When it comes to eroticism
I feel flamboyantly free
There are levels to all things intimate
I want you to explore them
Open your mind
Close your legs
I want all things imagined
To be written on these walls
With your love calls
Rebranding my brain
With the syllables of sexual tension
Adjectives of anticipation
Paragraphs of passion
Essays of ecstasy
A formation of fantasies
To soak through the pages of this book
Writing the wettest sheets
Saturating my soul
Made me lose all control
Now that I am in a different state of mind
I can give more
Go deeper
Go to places unseen
Just imagine reading
Expressing
All the things you will not say
Sensual suppression
Leaving you with words unspoken

Sticky Sheets

Is it too hot to make love?
I think not
Especially when I am here with you
Now lay back and relax
Steady your breathing
Turn on the box fan
Let the breeze meet the curves of your body
Let your anticipation grow
You have no clue of what you are in store for
Sweet sticky love juices
Dripping from you
Oh, you thought it was too hat
How could that be
When temperature should never play a factor
In the moment that I am sharing with you
Taking the time to taste you
Kiss you
Becoming one with you
Sending your body into spasms
Your muscles fighting a continuous war
Between cramps and relaxation
Just know I am here to satisfy your every need
That craving which has taken over your senses
Dripping this ice over your hot flesh
Making you anxious
Wanting to know what is going to happen next
Tilt your head back
Open your mouth
Let this cold liquid hydrate you
As I let the ice water drip between your chocolate hills
To the oasis that has been dry
since last night tricks and thrills
You arch your back to meet the trail
that is dripping between your thighs
I give you a break
As I go to get the biggest ice cube
Putting it in my mouth
Before kissing your knees

Unspoken Words

By

Makala Taylor

Straight darting down to your ankles
As I reach your toes
I take a brief intermission
Giving each toe special attention
Hearing you moan
I whisper
Shhhh
Not yet
Before kissing your lips
Giving you a perfect collab of hot and cold
You start moaning even more
Shhhh
Not yet
Walking around to the foot of the bed
Crawling slowly between your thighs
Getting ready to give you this summertime head
Drawing slow gentle circles around your clit
A squeal escapes from your lips
You are arching your back
To meet my licks
I pause to put an ice cube in my mouth
Bringing a little chill to you down south
I look up at you and tell you to cum for me
Fingers and toes clenched into the bed
You let out a moan
Then a scream
Squirting on my tongue
I get the best of both worlds
Warm and cold liquid pleasure
Swallowing every drop
As I slow down my kisses on your lips
I hear you say
Summer days are hot but worth it
It is just the sticky sheets
That I regret

Black Satin Sheets

It is the perfect night for a sleep over
I have been thinking about you all day
It started with a daydream
Before I knew it, I was soak and wet
Damn
The realness of it was so intense
But tonight, I am doing to make it a reality
Ambience is set
This will be a night you will not forget
Table set
Candles lit
I have cooked your favorite meal
In the background I have your favorite playlist playing
Its about to go down
A knock at the door
I open it
To find you standing there
Candy apple red dress
Heels to match
I take your hand and escort you in
You look around the room slowly smiling
Secretly knowing what is up
Walking you to the table
Pulling out your chair
As you get settle into it
I pour you a glass of wine
The atmosphere is so passionately intense
I feel you staring me down from across the table
I take some of my food and feed it to you
As you take your dessert later to do the same
The we hear the weather change outside as it begins to rain
We move our night into the living room
Caressing your hair
As I get caught up on your day
All the while you are talking
I massage your temples
Moaning you grab my hand
Resting it upon your chest

If this is a test
I am about to fail it proudly
Sliding it down to your breast
Drawing circles around your nipples
I see you are squirming under the pressure
Trying to hold on to your inhibitions
But right now, I am having a vision
Of me caressing your face with my hands
Kissing you
As you take my bottom lip captive between your teeth
You know that drives me crazy
We made out for a long time
To the point that I can no longer take it
I get up and tell you to come with me
I have a surprise with you
I blindfold you with the tie from my shirt
Directing you to my room
I take the blindfold off
Revealing to you
A room of intimacy and romance
Essential oils dancing in the air
Black satin sheets on my bed
Candlelight dancing around the room
I start to slowly undress you
I see the surprise that you had waiting for me
Red lace boy shorts
Looking exquisite against your caramel frame
You start undressing me
Kissing my neck
In that moment
I smell the wetness
That is collecting between my chocolate thighs
Creating a creamy surprise
Dropping to your knees
You shove your face firmly into it
Oh my God
The lethal weapon sliding from your lips
Into mine
I cannot help but to grab the back of your head
Shoving you deeper into my chocolate fold
The more you lick

The more my legs tremble
You are holding on to me tight
Making sure that I do not fall over
Licking harder and faster
Driving my body insane
Inflicting this lustful pain
I climax so hard
Arching my back
Pulling your dreads
Begging you to stop
As always that is a waste of time
You have gotten a taste
You are officially hooked on my love juices
Releasing your dreads
You come up to kiss me
The smell of me
Is intoxicating my senses
Now
It is my turn
To set your body a blaze
As you take your rightful place on my face
Giving you a heighten pleasure
That you started with me
I pick you up
Placing you on the edge of the bed
Kissing a trail from your forehead
Down to your lips
Moving to your bellybutton
Pacing myself slowly
To the honeypot that drips for me
Inserting my key
Unlocking the gate to heaven
Lying between your caramel thighs
Hypnotized by the way your hips synchronize
With each lick from my tongue
Taking you to a place
That runs parallel between passion and desire
Setting your body on fire
Trying to close your legs
To eject me from you
But I got you on lock down

So, you might as well calm down
I got you on lock down
Allow me to finish
What I have started
Jerking and bucking
Riding my face
Limpness is taking over your body
As I drain you of every ounce of energy
Full…satisfied…and naked
Holding one another
The sun is coming up
The candles have burned out
The playlist has come to an end
The only reminiscence of our night
Is our DNA soaked into these black satin sheets

Red Satin Sheets

As I watch you sleep
I cannot help but to think about
Just how sexy your chocolate skin looks
Intertwined with my red satin sheets
It was not too long
That you were screaming bloody murder
Clenching the sheets
As I drove you insane
Curling your toes
Trying to squeeze my head
Between your thighs
I must confess
I love the way you roll your hips
Grinding your clit
Against my lips
Breathing harder and faster
You are trying to regain control
Trying hard not to squirt
Leaving traces of your creamy nectar
Trying to roll me over
Trying to find some type of escape
Quickly learning there is none
You have only given me a better angle
For my tongue to fuck your pussy
Showing you that your pussy is mine
As you feel all five inches of my tongue
I want you to ride this anaconda
That you have released from its cave
Satisfy the feeling
The urge
The craving only, you can fulfill
Cum for me once more
Until all your juices flood my throat
Curing the desire
The burning fire that is deep inside of me
Body shaking
With each lick of my tongue

Now I am done
You can relax
Collapse onto the bed
There is nothing left to be said
Pussy aroma lingering on my lips
Just evidence left behind from your honeypot drips
Which has soaked right through my red satin sheets

White Satin Sheets

Walking into my room
Red velvet ropes
White satin sheets
Seeing that thirst that is read in your face
You have no clue what you are in store for
I have a treat just for you
Your favorite champagne
Chilling on ice
I am about to show you
What happens when you are a good girl
I know that you are anticipating every move that I make
All you need to know is that it is about to go down
What is about to take place tonight can
Can only be seen on Cinemax
So, relax there is nothing to be shy about
As I pull your hair
Kiss your lips
I hear you moan
I cup your breast in my hands
Pinching both nipples
You winch from the pressure applied
The smell of your love juices is starting to linger
I can tell you are about to explode
But I am not ready for my fun to end
Laying your body down on these white satin sheets
Hmmm
Open for me
Let me make your body my playground
By the end of the night
I want to have explored every part of you
It is a win for everybody
Kissing and licking your clit firmly
You let out a blood curdling scream
Telling me to keep going
Do not stop
Your clit is so hard
That it looks as if it is going to pop
When it does, I have my mouth in place to catch it all

Not letting one drop fall
Inserting a finger to massage your g-spot
The temperature is rising
From warm to hot
I refuse to stop
My hands are so sticky from your cream
Hmmm
Yes
I feel you getting close to the point of climax
Moaning
Thinking that when I am finished
That you are going to get payback
I do not think so
I plan on eating you right to sleep
Now ride this tongue until you are satisfied
Grinding your hips
Feeling in control
Invading your lips
Hmmm
Yes
We are almost there
Pull on my hair
Hmmm
Yes
I am getting closer
I am about to make you bust
Hmmm
yes
Getting closer
Legs tightening around my head
Hmmm
Yes
Cum now
Cum for me
Scream for me
Hmmm
Yes
You taste so sweet
You collapse next to me
I run mt fingers through your hair
Smiling so sweet

I watch you drift off to sleep
Thinking to myself
Who needs a late-night treat
When I have someone sweet like you to eat
As you look like milk and cookies
Wrapped in my white satin sheets

Imagine That

Imagine a day and time
When I am yours
And you are mine
Closing the space between us
You in your Tim's
Strapped up tight
I can see in your eyes what you want
I can tell that you are ready to punish this pussy
I mean damn Daddie
The way you control my body
With each stroke
Amazes me
I cannot help but to wait
The dominate way
You pull my hair gripping my hips
Smacking my ass
Making me drip
All over your caramel colored dyck
Hmmm
Sending me over the edge
Making me beg
For that ultimate pleasure
Licking on my back
Plunging deeper into this wet pussy
Grinding
Making me squirm
Making me hot
Begging
Damn Daddie
Do not stop
I am about to explode
From the inside out
Feeling my body shake
Breaking into a deep sweat
Sheets becoming wet
Can you imagine that?
Us together

Giving and receiving pleasure
Beyond measure
Stimulation of an immaculate imagination
Have me imagining
What just happened is not a dream
But a raw form of reality

Imagine This

Imagine a day and time
Caressing your imagination
You are stimulating my mind
Whispering those sensual words to me
Closing my legs
Squeezing them together
The distance between reality and my subconscious
Becoming more intense
In the frame of my mind
To dominate my body
It is I who will dominate yours
Have you gasping for air
Ripping out your hair
Ready to punish your pussy
Tongue lashing of a lifetime
Tonight, I am your daddie
Sending your body into spasms
Of multiple orgasms
Losing control with each stroke
From my anaconda tongue
I have just begun to have you sprung
On this anaconda tongue
Anticipating the aggressive way
You grab the back of my head
Pushing my face deeper into your pussy
Sucking and smacking my lips together
Feeling your pussy
Jump and thump under the pressure
Making you squirt
All over my face
Tasting the sweetness of you
The essence of you
Hmmm
How sweet it is
Flooding your sugar walls
Your body calling
For more satisfaction

My reaction
Is sending you over the edge
Making the beg
For the ultimate pleasure
Kissing the crack of your ass
Making you melt
Plunging deeper into your soaked pussy
Grinding and winding
Finding your G-spot
Making you squirt
Moaning
Daddie do not stop
Listen to that pussy pop
Feeling your body shake
As if I am in earthquake
Telling me
You are about to explode
Wrapping your legs around my head
Riding my tongue
Feeling your body relax
Breaking into a sweat
Now imagine that
Stimulation beyond measure
Engulfed in the reason
Of never ending passion

When I Think of Home

When I think of home I think of a place
Where your energy is overflowing
Your legs go from knocked to bowing
Your back scratches
Leaving an imprint that glows ruby red
I am not used to it
But now I have a heart
That is making me beg
Making me plead
Making me realize
That home is where I want to be
No need to fear
I will be gentle
I will give you courage
To endure the unknowing
With me you never know
When I think of home
I think of a place
Where your fat monkey
Flies high above my face
Preparing to ride it
Twin souls
Twin flames
Giving each other brain savagely
As I think in my mind
That you cannot win
Even though I feel you
Trying to hold in the passion within
You can try and click your heels together
Try to wish yourself out of this predicament
Just know that I got you
I will hold you steady
I will make sure that you are ready
Ready to make my bed
Your permanent residence
So, when I tell you to think of home
you will think of a place
where you never have to ask to see the wiz

he is strapped up
strapped on and ready to
make you think about home
making your sugar walls overflow
so, when I think of a place
I think of that place with our love is in it

Eat Me

Tease me
Please me
Ride me
Strap me
Hump me
Grind on me
Lick me
Suck me
Fuck me
Make love to me
Kiss me
Choke me
Bite me
Spank me
Love me
Hate me
Talk shit to me
Moan for me
Finger me
Penetrate me
Drink me
Taste me
Scream for me
Cum for me
Drip for me
Squirt for me
Ravage me
Devour me
Beast me
But more than anything
Make sure you eat me

Sweet Tooth

I have a craving
it is not for food
I have an urge
that needs to be fulfilled
But only you can do it
Your creamy middle
is sending me into a tailspin
Spread your legs
Let me in
The scent of your wetness
Draws me more into you
You taste so sweet
I cannot help but to dive in deeper
Deeper into your pleasure box
Getting hotter
As your moan's groans and grunts
Become squeal whines and screams
Slurping
Licking
Sucking
Flicking
Until the wave of orgasm rushes over you
Floods out of you
Into my mouth
Hmmmm
Damn
That hits the spot
The craving
The urge
The want
The need has been fulfilled
Ridding me of this sweet tooth

Pussy Sundae

Unpeel the banana
Place it between your lips
Tonight, you are my bowl
My tongue is the spoon
Scooping ice cream
Off your pussy
Making sure to lick it clean
Cold and hot sensations
Surging and merging
with the organic cream
That drips from your lips
A caramel drizzle
That will leave my lips a sticky mess
A mountain of whipped cream
Being slurped off every inch of you
You will be cumming soon
Howling at the moon
As you enjoy the fact
That you became my Pussy Sundae

Chocolate Drops

Your chocolate brown eyes
That make my vision pause
Your smile makes all convo worth while
The confidence that escape without haste
Informs me that you are ready for me
To caress you
Kiss you
Make love to you
Watching the chocolate drops
That forms from your chest
My lips gladly partake
Licking it
Savoring the very essence of you
Do not be afraid
Embrace what we can be
We deserve each other
Let us not look no further
We were meant to be together
Totally open and free

Chocolate Kisses

Chocolate Kisses
Leaving a trail
Through your mind
Loving
Embracing
Every inch of your frame
Shuttering and shivering
As I make love to your mind
My words becoming one
With your mental inhibitions
Making it known
You are mine
I am yours
Anyone who came before us
Had their time
Now it is our turn
To learn what love means
To love back who loves us
Giving their all
Not taking any slack
As I take the time to write about us
Let my chocolate kisses
Caress your soul
As I make love to you
Through my poetry

Caramel and Chocolate

I knew from the moment I saw you
That you would complement me
Like I would complement you
Two individuals so different
Yet the same
It is sad really
How you make me melt
From the mention of your name
Sweet and sincere in all that you do
It is no surprise
That after a year with you
I would fall for you
First discreetly
Now completely
Your chocolate goodness has my mind gone
You kissing me has my body tingling
Moaning has become our song
Your full lips
Wide hips
Love handles
Big breast
Do not intimidate me
Do not cover it up and let me see
What you look like totally naked
Not by the physical sense
But mental
Release all the pain from your past
It is temporary
We are going to make us last forever
Do not be fooled by my chunky chocolate frame
You know I am cocky
Conceited and confident
But you have broken me
I now take my time
To experience new things
Like writing this poem just for you
Though there are no words

That could describe my thoughts and feelings
But I will say this
My Chocolate body will melt onto yours
Seeing love in our hearts
Is such a beautiful thing
A work of art

Sugar Walls

Is it cake that you are baking?
If not
Whatever it is smell sweet
A mixture of vanilla fields and caramel syrup
I probably should not distract you
But I know you have thirty minutes to spare
I plan to make the most of it
Lifting you onto the counter
I knew you did not have any panties on
Making it easy to have access to you
Reaching to turn off the phone
We do not need any interruptions right now
I want your pussy attention
Yes, you heard me right
Now lay back
Let me quench my thirst
Sucking on your juice box
Feeling your clit swell
Becoming sensitive from the pleasure you are feeling
Then after I am finished
It will be my face that you will be riding
Burying my head between your legs
Proceeding to eat you
Like my favorite dessert
You are jerking as I slurp
Flicking my tongue over your clit
Sucking your pussy dry
Not missing one drop
You whisper not to stop
I know you are nearing completion
As your liquid glaze floods out of your sugar walls
Your body calls out for pleasure
Licking faster and deeper
Inserting my tongue into you
Scooping out all your sugary goodness
Hmmm
Slurping one more time

You squirt all over my face
Hmmmm
Swallowing hard
Clit still in my mouth
You are cumming so hard
Screaming so loud
You were so busy cumming
We never knew the timer for the cake went off
We quickly finish up
You can check on it
You put it on the cooling rack
Turn the lights off
Come to bed so that I can finish
Icing your cake

My Addiction

Your chocolate eyes
sucks me into you
Your caramel thighs
drawing me closer
Your strawberry lips
making me yearn for more
An ocean of sweat
rushing over me
You have my attention with each word you speak
My anticipation of holding
Caressing and kissing you
Has my nerves on edge
Needing to plunge deeper into you
You are my addiction
I need my fix
The words that flow from me
Are for you
You are my pusher woman
My strength
My weakness
My addiction
You say I have you
Yet it is you who has me
Impatiently waiting to see you
Touch you
Be one with you
My heart
My mind
My body
My imagination runs wild
Just with the thought of being with you
My addiction might be you
But soon the addiction will be ours
You may not know it yet
But you will be hooked on me
Just as I am hooked on you
An addictive urge

You are wanting me
Like a shark needing to feed
I can see the urge to feed
It is all in your eyes
Besides the body never lies
You know you want me
So bad now that you can taste it
Now receive it
Eat it
Drink it
Touch it
Crave it
But whatever you do
Do not waste it

Pussy Overdose

When I see it
I must fight the feeling
To eat it
To smell it
To look at it
To lick it
To stick it
To become one with it
To kiss it
To make love to it
It is the only addiction that I have ever had
When I cannot have it
I get moody and mad
I cannot help feeling this way about pussy
The beautiful way it sits between your legs
Making me want to relapse each time
Especially when it is fresh out the shower
Smelling like your favorite body wash
Biting my lip
Seeing you naked
Wanting to bend you over
To eat you from the back
Thinking I am being dramatic
When I tell you how badly I want it
I know the longer I go without it
The longer I will eat it when I get it
Overdosing on it once again
Only this time stopping myself
Before going insane on it
My pussy addiction can and will be controlled
If I let myself do so
Turning Me On
It is the look in your eyes
The sway of your thighs
That makes my heart race
Could it be the style of your hair?
The perfume you wear

That set fire to my desire
Drunk with passion
The satisfaction of knowing you are the shit
The haters will hate
You are not caring one bit
You know who you are
You know who I love
I see you dread your hair
Picking out something to wear
You stop and stare at me
I feel completely open
Raw with emotions
Never spoken
Always listening to my body language
What I see in you in us is imperfectly perfect
What makes us work
Having the confidence to know
What others say do not matter
What we feel for each other
Does turn me on
You will always be my addiction
I will always overdo it
Falling into a coma
From this pussy overdose

Mental Stimulation

Penetrating my wildest of dreams
Most erotic fantasies
I know you want to see me
Breathe me
Become one with me
Setting yourself free
As I strip you naked with my words
Caressing your body with my eyes
Letting time fly
As we make music only the way we can
Telling me how you like it
Telling me that you are ready to come
Oh, how I love how your body reacts
Just from listening
To my mental masturbation
A Manipulation
Of your imaginary stimulation
Now touch me where only you can
As we sub come to this mental stimulation

Ear Hustler

I am sitting in the Living room
Earphones on trying hard not to listen
Trying hard not to get turned on
The moans and groans I hear in the far distance
Are so intense
So sexy
The Sucking sounds
Sounds of pure wetness
Is making my hormones react
Making my own juice box squirt
Do not mind me pretend I am not here
Take that toy out please each other with it
Many may call it awkward
I call it adventurous and sexy
Now as y'all reach y'all peak
I hear the headboard banging
Bedsprings squeaking
Toes curling
Heavy breathing
Trying hard not to release your love call
But your stubby not having that
She licks
She sucks
I hear you release
Her release
Now I have released
Hmmm
Who knew you could climax without touching yourself
But when you ear hustle
It is amazing all the things that could be heard
All things heard I thoroughly enjoyed
I must say stud for stud is sexy as hell
Thank y'all
For taking my imagination on a sexual vacation
From my mind to y'all bedroom
It was truly a trip I shall never forget

Tonight

Tonight, is the night
That you breathe life into my body
Pumped oxygen in this empty vessel
Intravenously infuse my body with passion and desire
Before tonight
I was the walking dead of disappoint and resentment
Before tonight
I was Angry and bitter
Tonight, nothing matters
All that matters is the heat
That radiates from between your legs
To meets the fire
That protrudes from my lips
Moans of satisfactions
My back
Being branded with the scratches
We are in the coldest room in the house
Yet
Sweat drips from our bodies
My eyes scan your naked canvas
Longing for a good tongue lashing
Do not run
Do not hesitate
Just lay back
Let me taste your sweet nectar
That drips from your sugar walls
Barely touching it
and yet you are singing our favorite song
Moans
Groans
Oohs and ahhs
Feeling your legs shake
Causing the bed to tremble
You arch your back
Trying to get your body to relax
But it is too late
Your body has forsaken you

Riding the waves of orgasms
Body spasms
Clenched hands gripping the sheets
Curled up feet
Trying to catch your breath
Tonight, I want you breathless
Motionless
Thoughtless
Senseless
As I make you remember everything you forgot
Tonight, we are going to combine our bodies
Making our presence known
Enjoying what was
What is
What will be us
For our time has come to an end
We came as lovers
Tonight, we are leaving as friends

One Night of Passion

What started as a night of work
Ended as a night of passion
We made some of the sweetest love ever
One kiss on my breast made my body shake
One lick of my nipple made me melt
I sat on your lap and felt myself
Continuously explode again and again
Feeling you dive in and out of me
Driving me crazy with anticipation
The way you picked me up
Making me feel so sexy and desired
The way you made love to me
I can say it was the best I ever had
Sweet and sweaty love making is always considered
To be the best of all time
The way you held me
Positioned me and handled me
Letting me know how much you missed me
Love me and cared for me
From the bottom of my heart
I want to tell you
I love you
Thank you for making me feel so desired
Sexy and loved

A Night of Pleasure

You pick me up from work
Instead of going home
You took me to dinner
We had deep conversation
Our eyes met in a very intense manner
We were trying to read each other's mind
Our hands meet in the middle of the table
As if we were preparing to tango
Better yet the forbidden dance
Our fingers curved in the most intimate way
Feeling my foot slide up and down your leg
Slowly arousing you
Instead of going to the movies
We go back home
For a night of passion and stimulation
Not only physically but mentally
That is when a night of passion
Turned into a night of pleasure

Intimate Phenomenon

From the moment I met you
 I could tell you was different
From the deepness of your voice
To the calming way you carried yourself
I could not help it
My feelings became intense quickly
Now they are spiraling out of control
Taking a toll on the tender part of me
Piercing me with the double edge sword
That I know as your tongue
Now the pain has begun
The tears now burn my face
Every time they fall
I call your name in my dream
Only for you not to answer
But I awaken to realize
It is not a dream
But reality
That has sunk in
I wish, hope, and dream for you to be with me
But that will never happen
I am no longer your cup of tea
You like a different brand
A stronger brand
One that is not so sweet
But bitter
It is funny how things change
But the more I dwell on it
The more my chest hurts
The more my heart aches
I sometimes wish I were numb
Cold
Unfeeling like I used to be
But you broke me
Only to remold me
Into the very thing you cannot stand
An emotional being

One that feels every word
That you throw at me
I wish I were free
From the torture
That I will forever feel
That is imprisoned in my heart
But at this point I am focused on me
The future that is laid out in front of me
So, thank you for the pain
You have made me the person I am today

Pure Ecstasy

Hot summer nights
Spent waiting
Anticipating
Longing
For the touch of you
Taste of you
Hearing your sweet voice
Whispering what you would
What you could do
If you were here
Near me
Pleasing me
Teasing me
Wanting me
Needing me
To kiss you until all gravity becomes nonexistent
Causing that tingle up your spine
Taking my time
To make your body mine
Have you reached ecstasy yet?
Are you waiting for me to penetrate your imagination?
Sparing no expense on caressing thoughts
I love the way your subconscious
Your lyrical words
Melts into mine
A game of mental tag
First, you are it
Your play on words
Reading my eyes
For the gateway to my soul
Is opening to you with no hidden surprises
Now I am it
Finishing the game
Driving you insane
With the drips
That fall from my lips
Saturating your earlobes

Making you soaked
Making you wet
To never forget
What it is that you came here for
Could it be for the fun conversation
Sexual contemplation
Mental stimulation
Only you know
But whatever brings you here
To play the game you play
Just know I play for keeps
I play to win
That being said
Open to me
Set your body free
Let me inside of you
To discover what really happens
When you let pure ecstasy take over

Wave of Ecstasy

I love the scent you give out
When you are wet
It is the sweetest fragrance
I will never forget
The taste of you
Is intoxicating
That when you are gone to long
I cannot help but to wait
To see you
Smell you
Taste you
Hear you
Feel you
You grab my head
Push me deeper into your pussy
Tell me it is mines
As I eat it without hesitation
Now let your legs rest upon my shoulders
Though you have came once
Cum again
As I have you riding the wave of ecstasy
Into the great abyss of passion and desire

Blood Boiling

Mental stimulation
Multiple observations
Of the person you were
The person you used to be
Your touch burning my skin
Releasing the fire from within
Yearning your kisses of passion
Being content enough to call your bluff
Licking a trail that will never dry
Flooding my oasis
Tasting the very part of me that is sweet
My clit and your tongue becoming one
As you trace your name on what is yours
I am branding your back
With stripes of uncontrolled actions
Brought on by satisfaction
That only you can provide
Now my blood is boiling
Rising straight to the top
Ready to pop
Do not stop
Hmmmm
Now my blood boils
Heart races
For the uncontrollable urge that has been met

A Journey of Stimulation

Pack your emotional bags
Let me take you on a trip
A trip that is sure to end
At a point of no return
Watch me as I approach you
Feel me as I touch you
Caress you
Give you roaming fingers
Chasing hands
Squeezing
Touching every part of you
Feeling me breathe on your neck
As I grind on you
Hmmmm
The scent from your perfume
Taking my senses on a journey
One I do not want to come back from
You have my lips wanting
Needing
To taste every part of you
Everything from your nipples
That rises
Just from one look from me
To your sweet
Hot and sticky
Creamy middle that waits just for me
Cannot you see what you do to me
Have me on my knees
Ready to drink
Every drop of sweet nectar from you
Becoming full of your overflowing juice box
My tongue is steadily going up and down your clit
Separating the split
That holds your sweet oasis
Let my tongue proceed to skinny dip in it
Becoming one with it

It is then that I feel you
You are trying to escape
From the pleasure you feel
Questioning is this a mirage
Is it real?
Ride the tsunami of orgasm
As it rushes over you
Washing over you
Silent screams becoming louder
Pushing my head to tell me to stop
Pulling my hair to tell me to keep going
Back arching
Legs shaking
I watch as you try to breathe through it
Instead of admitting that you just cannot take it
You finally start to calm down
Quietness fills the space we are in
Your legs collapse
Sweet whispers of I love you exchanged
Quickly followed by a kiss
Now who ever thought
That a journey between two strangers
Two lovers would end up like this

M.O.D.

Stiletto heels
Always completed your outfit
It is concealing tonight's meal
You are my feast
Which is wrapped up in fishnet stockings
Giving you that dominatrix look
That I am craving
Make me your sex slave
Tell me how to please you
With my teeth
I am removing your black lace panties
Revealing what keeps me coming back for more
Role playing the part of a junkie
You are my supplier
Give me my fix
Take me and make me high
Pussy crack is what you are supplying
Ripping you out of your dress
Kissing you
Bringing you to a place
That is parallel to desire and passion
Taking my tongue
Caressing every curve
You have been blessed with
I want your body to be my playground
My amusement park
My slip and slide
To ride all I want
Skinny dipping into your cleavage
My lips getting submerged
Engulfed in your chocolate covered mountains
I love how your nipples call me
I cannot help but to answer
With a simple lick
You moan
I brush your hair out of my path
Feeling your breathing quickening

The pressure from my tongue
Made you kick off your heels
Wrap your legs around me
Pulling me closer to you
Nibbling
Sucking
Biting on your nipples
They are so hard now
I can smell your wetness
Damn it smells so inviting
So intoxicating
I want to partake in you
Get lost in you
Lick a trail
With each flick of my tongue
I feel you exhale
Your manicured fingertips
Pulling my hair
Pushing me to eat you
Taste you
Explore your insides with my tongue
The pleasure has begun
I take the tip of my tongue
I start writing my name on your pussy
Starting with the R
You try and compose yourself
Then A your moans heighten
Then V-E-N
Quickly being whipped across your lips
The more I lick
The more your hips buck
The more I flick
The more you grind
The more you hump my face
I take your legs
Placing them on my shoulders
Locking your legs down
Diving my tongue deeper
Hearing your moans become screams
Cumming for me
Back to back

Moans becoming light whimpers and whines
Until the feeling leaves you
Leaving you numb
Leaving me full
The M.O.D. has struck again
Set up your next appointment
Let the fun begin

Head Doctor

You say you have an ache
That you cannot get rid of
An urge
A craving
That has consumed you
You call me to make an appointment
The feeling has become unbearable
I set it for that night
Just make sure to leave all doubt at the door
For what I have waiting for you
Is sure to satisfy you
Step into my office
Take your clothes off
Let me examine you
I look at your nipples
They do not seem to be responding
They are normally hard
I take an ice cube
Rub it all over
Squirming from the coldness of it
Moaning from the pleasure of it
I tell you to open your legs
Seeing if the dryness you reported has been fixed
You are hesitate at first
I continue to rub your nipples
Pinching them gently
Your legs separate
I look
You are beginning to produce wetness
But not enough
So, I take my finger
Slowly insert it into you
Feeling you tightening around it
Continuing to slide my finger in and out
Until I hear the wetness rushing from you
I ask are you still in pain
You reply yes unbearable pain

I tell you to point to it
Putting one finger in your mouth
Quickly pointing to your clit
Still massaging your g-spot
I take my mouth and blow on it
You moan louder
Noting your actions
Pulling my finger out
I take a towel wipe away your wetness
That you created
Now let us cure this ache that you are feeling
I kiss your clit
While doing that
I suck on it
As I pull away
It is starting to swell
I take my tongue and lick it
I hear you squealing
I lick harder and faster
Your squirming and heavy breathing
Let me know if I am on the right spot
To improve matters further
I take your nipples
Rub my fingers over them
Once harden
I pinch them
Still slurping
Licking
Sucking
Flicking
Your body starts going into convulsions
Bucking
Jerking
Your hands clinching the sheets
I keep licking
Tongue fucking your pussy
Aggressively each time down
On the 10th time up
You silently scream
But me licking your clit harder
You release the scream

You were holding back
Followed by whining
I ask do you want
Need me to stop
You whine no do not stop
So, I keep going
Until all sense of reality is no more
All feeling from your pussy is nonexistent
Now your body is relaxing
Your breathing is getting back to normal
I am standing up looking over your sweaty body
I ask has all your ailments been cured
Pausing in between breaths
You reply HELL YES
I am glad I was able to cure your ache
The inflammation burning deep within
Now my only question is
Do you want to set up another appointment?
The Head Doctor is always busy
So, you must plan ahead
To get this fiyah head

Black Lips

Your lips spit hot fire
Of desire and passion
Releasing a tongue
That is sure to give my love button a lashing
I cannot help but to run
When I see your black lips
Pursuing me
I know I am only making it harder on myself
I am going to lay back
Wrap my legs around your head
Beg you for completion
As the secretion of pleasure
Pour out of my sugar walls
Sending my body into spasms
Of multiple orgasms
That is not easy to control
Making sure to show me what your black lips are about
With each lick I jerk
With each slurp I start squirting
All over your face
Giving you a taste of my sweet nectar
My legs tighten around your head
As I Beg you to stop
Not knowing English
You keep going until you have licked me clean
Leaving no evidence behind of this night to be seen
On your sheets
Licking my juices from your black lips
Thinking to yourself
Damn
Bae you told me you were sweet enough to eat
You were right

Trip Down South

Your pink lips
Soft and wet
Taste so sweet
Why do I need dessert
When it is you that I want to eat
Your body so soft
My tongue glides across it so easily
Sucking your chocolate chip nipples
Will be sending your body into a frenzy
Pushing them together licking them simultaneously
Watching you melt right before my eyes
Kissing you deeply
Sucking your bottom lip
Moans escaping you
I feel you rocking your hips
I smell your sweet creamy cum
I cannot help but to run my hand
In between your thighs
Diving hand first into your oasis
The sound of your wetness is taking a toll
While my finger plunge deeper into your hole
The scratches on my back is driving me
Removing my finger
Replacing it with my tongue
Now it is time for some fun
I am slurping
I am licking on your pussy
It was at that moment
That your moans
Became whimpers of passion
Screams quickly following each tongue lash
You are pulling on my braids
Which makes it worse for you?
Now my tongue is forced to invade you
Persuade you
To open wider
So, I can go deeper

Sucking the cum out of your abyss
You cum so hard
It squirts all in my mouth
Making me glad that I took the trip down south
If every night is like tonight
You are going to make me happy to miss my flight

A Trip Back Down South

No talking required
Just come in
Take off your clothes at the door
Letting your boxers hit the floor
Pushing you against the wall
Roughly kiss your lips
As I grind my hips against yours
Your hand finding its way into my panties
My mouth devouring your breast whole
Clenching your nipples between my teeth
Moans falling from your mouth
As I take a trip back down south
Licking your wet slit
It tastes so sweet
I shove my tongue into your honey pot
Flooding your sugar walls
With the sweet nectar that flows within
Caused by the pleasure and passion
That collides with our fire and desire
That sparks up every time we are together
No matter the situation or weather
The only thing that matters is that
When you cum
You cum hard and long
If not
I am going to keep licking and sucking
Flicking
Finger fucking
Until your legs shake
Hips grinding and rotating
Trying to maintain composure
Going Slowly
Until every drop of moisture drips
From your honey pot onto my tongue
Collapsing onto the sofa
Out of breath
Exhausted and motionless

Realizing that sometimes getting to the point
Is all that is needed and required

To my Stud King

My chunky studking
I love the way you devour me
Sex is good
Head is amazing
Your tongue is hypnotizing
Soft and Wet
Your tongue tasting this sweet peach
That drips just for you
It is a waterfall that drowns you
As I ride your face
Grip my hips
As I grind my lips on your lips
The way you make me feel
The way you make me squeal
My clit at its hardest
Each lick and flick of your tongue
Is making me think of that time
We made love on our hardwood table
How when you pulled down your dickie pants
You revealed a strap
That was waiting for me to suck
Making it so wet
That when you slide it in
I would bust it open for you
Putting my legs up
Pushing them over my head
Making me beg for more
Deeper
Harder until we cum together
Dripping all over the table
Sharing a kiss
That must be nothing but pure bliss
I love hot and steamy days like this
You show me just how much I am missed

Sexual Haiku

I love the feel of your skin
So soft to the touch
Feeling like the softest silk
Eyes that I can get lost in
Gateways to your soul
Making me melt from within
I can kiss your lips all day
For they taste so sweet
Sucking your lips so gently
Kissing a trail down your neck
Licking your nipples
You squirm under the pressure
Playing in my hair
Branding my back with love marks
Hearing your love call
Sucking gently on your clit
Damn you taste so sweet
Absolutely delicious
You are my dessert
Licking your creamy goodness
Now your thighs are tight
Flicking sucking and licking
I feel you lose it
Now your river flows for me
Do not fight the feeling
This is your night of passion
Lay back and enjoy
Feeling your breathing slow down
I stop to kiss you
Asking you guess what I have done
You smile at me and say what
I simply reply
I made you run was not that fun

Sexually Combine

It was a matter of chance
It started with a glance
Running my fingers through your hair
Pulling your head back intensely
Kissing and nibbling on your neck
Moans escape you
I slide my hands down your pants
Heat radiating from your pussy
I navigate until I find your clit
Twirling my finger around
Stroking up and down
Do not you make a sound
You are biting your lip
Clawing at my back
I feel your legs buckle
Like they are becoming detached
I make you sit in this chair
Open wide
Let me stick my tongue
In the deepest part of you
Longing to drink from you
My head bobbing up and down
Moving round and round
As I feel you squirming
Trying so hard not to make a sound
I stop
Straddle you in the chair
Thinking there was not any room
Undoubtingly there was
Underestimating the flexibility of your legs
Allowing our thighs to easily combine
The heat from our pussy
Feeling like a raging fire
Smelling the wetness from you still on my lips
Kissing you softly
Caressing you gently
Sucking on your nipples

As you link your hands in my dreads
Rubbing our clits together
We explode all over each other
Legs locked together
By the intensity we just shared
You came for me
I came for you
Now let us go take a shower
Grab a bite to eat
Preparing for round two

A Sexual Free Fall

Sweat pouring onto my body
From you riding me
Eyes glazed over
Hypnotizing smile
Lips that ooze pure sexual energy
Can I caress you like this?
Chocolate kisses on your caramel French tipped toes
You melt and squirm under the pressure
Of me kissing you gently
Becoming more serene
In depth with the way you squirm
Then quietness falls across the room
With only our heavy breathing remaining
Now the fun and games can now begin
Can I kiss you like this?
Giving your love button a long-wet kiss
Pulling my hair
Drawing me near to you
Closer to you
Becoming one with you
The taste of you drives me crazy
Why does your nectar intoxicate me?
Making me drunk with desire
I cannot think of a better way to express it
Than to taste it
Devour it
Ravage it
Licking it clean
This offers the sexual stimulation
That penetrates my imagination
Can I taste you like this?
Take me
Make me your sexual slave
Tie me up
Make me do any and everything to you
I would not do other wise
Take me and show me
The surprises that you behold

Becoming bolder with each movement
Rising and falling
Got my body calling time out
I know you are watering my garden
For it was dry
Now it is flooding
Can I dominate you like this?
Vibrations that ripples
From your hard nipples
To your creamy middle
A trail of fire being released from my tongue
Up to your caramel thighs
Awaiting your sticky surprise
Getting lost in your thickness
Making things become more intense
Setting my body a blaze
 From the mention of my name
Can I get lost in you?
Now you just showing off
Riding my face with no hands
Be careful not to fall off
Grind on me girl
As my tongue twirls
All over your clit
Passion growing with each lick and flick
Now my lips are glazed
With the sweet juices of passion
My body heat is soaking into the sheets
Now release that load from within
Can I drink you like this?
Forgetting how thin the walls are
The neighbors hear your love call
You collapse onto the bed
I kiss your forehead
Then your lips
Before whispering in your ear
"Was it as good for you as it was for me?"
Sighing you reply
"Yes, it's even better than I imagined"
I smile as I think to myself
You have not seen anything yet

Sexual Invasion

The love we about to make
Will be out of this world
From the way I kiss your lips
To the way I lick on your pearl
Keep your eyes on me
I do not want you to miss a thing
I want you to steady your breathing
As I flick my tongue ring on your clit
I feel your senses growing wilder and hotter
Trying to hold in the moans
They escape you
The intensity grows
As my tongue slither into your walls
Feeling your body call
For release from this heat
At that very moment
My tongue withdraws from you
Causing you to squirt all over my chin
Letting me know I win
That when you begin the fun
It will never end

Sexually Aggressive

I push you onto the bed
You pull my hair
I love it when you take control
Taking a toll on the very inner part of me
Kiss me rough
Fuck me rougher
Now let me flip you onto the bed
Burying my head
Between your legs
Making my mouth drop open
Hmmm
Do you like that?
Yeah
I passionately kiss your clit
With my lip's soft pecks
To make you wet
You squirm
As I release the beast from its cage
A long python or could it be an anaconda
That seeks to invade
Persuade you to open wider
Allowing me access to you
Inside you
To please you
Tease you
Feed from you
Drink from you
All the pleasure juice that drips from you
Making love to you with my tongue
Locking your legs down
I see you trying to run
I drag you to the edge of the bed
Burying my head deeper into you
Feeling you twitch with every lick and slurp
Damn you taste good
Better than ice cream
Licking and flicking your clit

Legs tensing up
Back arching
Toes curling
Now I feel you shaking
Bucking and jerking
Letting me know the moment is approaching
Then it happens
You throw your head back
Let out a blood curdling scream
Wrapping your legs around my head
Grunting
I keep eating you savagely
Finally, you squirt
Relaxing your legs from around my head
I crawl to kiss you
Your sweet nectar is all over my face
I watch you doze off
Thinking to myself
Damn
I am still hungry
I guess I will curl up next to you
Play in your hair until the sun rises
Leaving footprints across the morning sky

Sexual High

Every time we make love
I have the munchies
You make me so high
That the ground disappears
Gravity is no longer
The only thing that exist is our naked bodies
Sweaty and hot
Wet sheets
Which has been pulled from the bed
I lost all control as you were giving me head
It felt like I would never catch my breath
Come down from this sexual high that I felt
Kissing your lips as traces of me lingered
Taking my senses on a trip
Letting your hands do the walking
And your fingers do the talking
Talking in circles around my clit
Making me moan without hesitation
Quickly bringing me to the point of no return
Removing your finger
Replacing it with your tongue
I made reservations
To eat you out and I will not be late
Because I have been waiting to eat all day
Starving
Wanting
Needing
To ravage you
I am addicted to what is between your thighs
If there was rehab for pussy eating
I would need to admit myself
I will not lie
For you are my bad habit
That is hard to break
At this point I do not want to

Wet Dream

Lying in bed looking at the ceiling
Thinking to myself that I am in need
In need of what you may ask
A sexual healing
A healing that only can be explored
From the inside out
A cure that will leave me drained
Knocked the hell out
Shredded sheets
From gripping them tightly
A huge puddle
That will take days to dry
You may ask why
It is because of the constant licking
Sucking
Flicking
From the beast I call Anaconda
Making your mind wonder
Pondering about if it can get any better
If it can get any wetter
The answer is simple
Yes
Just put your legs upon my shoulder
As I get bolder in my pursuit of you
Of your treasure between your thighs
Taking my time
Making it mine
Sucking it dry
I want you to see all the things
Your body wants
Needs and craves
It can be well taking care of
In the matter of minutes
So lay back
Do not run
Get ready to have some fun
Feel free to moan

Feel free to scream
No one can hear you
Inside of this thing I call a wet dream

Quickie

Your body glistening and wet
From just taking your shower
You come in the room
Lay across the bed
You spread legs
Telling me
To show your pussy some love
Licking my lips
I kiss your clit
Slow and gentle
Feeling your pussy jump with each kiss
I lick and suck on your clit
Hmmm you taste so good
I slide my finger into you
Massaging your g-spot
Hmmm
The wet sounds coming from you
Is turning me on
Twirling my tongue all over your pearl
Slurping and sucking on your pussy
With trembling thighs
Rolling eyes
You cum for me making extremely happy
Do not stop me
Encourage me to give you the pleasure
You deserve want and need

Sexual Insanity

Sex may take me to paradise
But your words take me to a place
That is way beyond that
Giving my heart palpitations
Each time you touch my hand
Kiss my lips
Sending my subconscious on a sensual trip
That I desperately needed
Succeeding to take me
To the island of ecstasy
Never knowing that the fire
The desire that escape from me
Onto you would be untamable
Driving us both into our own sexual insanity
Ripping our clothes to shreds
Breaking the bed
Both of our bodies begging
For pleasure to be released
From its cage
Sending us into a rage
Now open and let me in
So, our vacation to sexual intimacy can now begin

Orgasmic Wave

Kissing the nape of your neck
You arch your back
To take this strap
To take this pounding
Do not run
Do not whine
Just bend over and give me what is mine
Let me take my time
Stroking you deep
Slapping that ass
Pulling your hair
Making you weep
While you are clawing at the sheets
Hmmm back it up on me
Putting you in the wheelbarrow position
Bout to catch a cramp
Flip over to your back
Give me those legs
So, I can push them back into the headboard
Slow grinding on you
Looking into your eyes
Kissing your soft lips
As I feel you gripping my hips
Pushing me deeper into you
See…
Why you make me bite you?
Feeling the passion between us intensify
This has me nibbling on your neck
You start moan even louder
I continue nibbling on your collarbone
Your moans become screams
As I make your pussy cream
Dripping all over my chocolate colored dyck
I feel your thighs tightening
It is drawing closer to that moment
We both about to bust
After you reached your peak

You were unable to speak
As you motioned for me
To come sit on your face
I took my rightful place
Upon my royal throne
The feel of your tongue
Stroking softly against my clit
Anticipating giving you my cream to drink
You are licking faster
Shoving your tongue deeper
Making me grip the headboard
Keeping me from falling on you
My love juice rushing from me
Down your throat
I am trying to run
You grip my hips
Locking me in place
I ride the orgasmic wave
Until no feelings are left
Collapsing next to you
Feeling exhausted and out of breath
I love the way our bodies feel together
I want to and we will stay like this forever

Dive In

Do not move on to the next girl
Just come to me
A woman
That will have you cumming
Have you spreading your legs
Making you beg for more
Do not try to lock the door now
For I have the key already
To stick it in
Just stay calm and steady
I can be your lover
Fuck buddy and friend
No need for pretending
That you do not want me
To put that fire out
Pleasing you is all I am about
Deep sea diving is what I am good at
Holding my breath for long periods
While I eat you
I know you will be thirsty when I finish
Just lay back
Let me quench your thirst
Tasting you has me in a state of mind
That I no longer want to take my time
Giving you the tongue lashing of a lifetime
You say you want wetness to be the result
Once I eat it up
I am going to strap up and beat it up
Bringing your fantasy to completion

Sexual Buffet

Wanting to take my time with you
To explore you
From the inside out
Strumming the pages of your sexual book
Trying every position
Kissing every nook
Caressing every cranny
Your body is my playground
Your breast is the hill
I want my tongue to roll down
Your thighs are hidden valley
I want my hands to slide down
Rushing back up
Allowing my fingers to skinny dip
In your hole
Watching you lose all control
Flooding my sheets
Hmmm
Damn you taste so sweet
You make me want to get lost in you
Become one with you
Kissing the very lips that drip for me
Making me realize just how wet you get
Wet sounds escaping from within
I knew once I started
It would be a while before it ends
That is fine by me
I was hungry anyway
My head is parked between your legs
My mouth is ready
For an all you can eat buffet

Prisoner of Passion

Walking down the hallway to my room
The anticipations building
You walk in
Take your clothes off at the door
Body looking like it belongs on the cover of playboy
You kiss my lips
The passion behind it brings me great joy
My nipples hardening
Pussy pulsating
Hmmm
The scent of you drives me crazy
Pulling that pussy onto my face
You feel my tongue running a race
Only I can win
Ride it
Grind on it
Do not run
Let me tame that pussy
Let me give you multiple orgasms
That is sending your body into spasms of pleasure
Toes curling
Hands gripping the sheets
Trying to get me off
I got you locked down
My tongue is making love to your pussy
Passionately tongue kissing your clit
Hmmm
Yeah
Grab my head
Push me deeper into your sugar walls
Tasting your love juices
As it drips down my tongue
Damn you taste so sweet
Making my meal complete
I have eaten your pussy
Now let me suck you dry
Making your pussy cry

Let me dry your pussy tears with my tongue
Hearing you whimper and whine
Faster and deeper
My tongue invades your pussy
Release all energy onto my face
Your love call echoing off the walls
I release you from my prison of passion
Seeing your body lose control
For the head I just gave you has taken its toll
On your mind, body, and spirit

Orgasmic Virgo

They call me Nympho Virgo
Always in the mood
To eat you up and strap you down
Not playing around with it
But straight kissing the clit
Lick the slit
That drips just for me
Got me waiting
Anticipating
Tasting your sweet love juices
As it flows from your oasis
Damn
I feel the intensity
Rippling up from your curled toes
To your tightening thighs
That is clenched around my head
I do not mind
Taking my time
Sending your body into spasms
Of multiple orgasms
That has the middle of the bed wet
How soon did you forget
We had an argument
You wanted to make love that morning
Because your body was
Wanting
Needing
Craving for me to put it out of its misery
But I would not
Now you want to be moody
Slamming doors
Giving me the silent treatment
But where is the silence now?
As I give you the tongue lashing of a lifetime
I feel you arching your spine
Releasing soft whines of pleasure
You grab a hold of my hair

As you do every time
That you are getting ready to cum
Pushing my face deeper into you
Humping my face
Grunting
Moaning
Screaming
Yelling for me
To eat my pussy
Indeed I will
Getting your mind right
By giving you that fiya head
Are you still moody?
No
Are you still Mad?
No
That just goes to show you
You can start the battle of attitudes
But I will always win the war of moods

Deja Vu

Bae do not look at me that way
You set my soul on fire
Got me burning with desire
The way you look at me
Right before we kiss
Makes me want moments like this
Not to end
But to give me steady moments of Deja vu
With you always leaving traces of your lipstick
On the tip of my clit
Making me forget
Where we were
What time it is
All I do know though
Are those bedroom eyes
Looking at me from between my thighs
Is sure to drive me wild
From beginning to end
Latching on the clit like a pacifier
Turning me from a moaner
To a screamer over night
You gave me déjà vu from the moment
You sucked my toes
Left hickies on my calves
Smacked my ass
Pulled my hair
Sucked my nipples
Tossed my salad
Only to circle back around
Finishing me off
Overflooding my abyss
Making it flood 7 days
7 nights down south

Sexual Cockiness

LMAO
Making me cry
Please
I will have you dropping to your knees
Ready to give me head
Pushing you on the bed
Raising your legs above your head
Dreads falling into your face
Locking you into place
Taking my five inches
Penetrating your pussy
The way my words penetrate your soul
Taking a toll on your body and imagination
Keeping you guessing
Wondering
What is next
Will you be able to withstand?
Sucking your toes
Air escaping through your nose
Sliding my finger in
Teasing and pleasing your G-spot
Making you sweat
Making you hot
Wanting me to stop
My cockiness exceeds me
Playing with your nipples
Feeling your body tremble
Under the pressure that is building
Teasing your mind
Pleasing your body
With my sexual cockiness

New Year Sex

It is New Year's true enough
I call your bluff
As you try to make me tap out
The nympho Virgo in me will not allow it
I am too aggressive to tame
To dominating to obtain
You wreck your brain
Trying to figure out
Why you are going insane
From the wild ride I am taking you on
You cannot help but to moan
Your toes popping
Throwing up gang signs
This hot throbbing pussy
Feeling so good it has you drooling
Mouth dropping open
This pussy will leave you speechless
Breathless with the skills and thrills
I provide so do not get it twisted
You may have me sweating
That does not mean you got me hooked

I am Hungry

I am craving you
Needing and wanting you
To curb this appetite tonight
I do not want to argue or fight
I just want to make love to your mind
While I fuck your pussy right
I do not want to play games
I do not play with my food
You are my prey
I hunt everyday
To eat
To partake
To devour
To ravage
Swallow in its entirety
You see it is my goal
To have your heart skip a beat
Sending vibrations through you
Before penetrating you
Telling you what I really want to do
Wanting to learn you
Study you
Explore you
When I am finished
I will have you losing control
Mind body and soul

Summer loving

It is raining outside
Flooding inside
Our bedroom
Humid from our workout
Laying here trying to catch your breath
But cannot because it is too hot
I pull the box fan out
Plug it in
Turning it on high
Now it is cooling down
You take a deep breath
Look at me
Stood up
Strapped up
Motioning
For me to come to you
Not knowing that heat could turn a person on
Seeing how hype you were to ram that
Tap that
Grab that
Smack that
Intrigued me to the point of no return
I was soak and wet
Before you even licked it
You went to eat it
To my surprise
I did not want it
I just wanted your strap
Making my legs buckle from one stroke
Wrapping my hair around your hand
Pulling it
While smacking my ass
Making it ripple
Loving it when you take charge
Throwing it back on you
Meeting the rhythm of your thrust
Releasing my hair

Gripping my hips
Feeling the sweat from you drip
All over me
You are grinding your strap deeper into me
My body reacting
You are hitting my walls
Making me scream
Making me cream
All over you
All over your strap
All over the bed
This makes you pump harder
My pussy throbbing and wet
Making me forget
Just how hot it is
But once we are all done
I collapse
Breathing fast yet steady
You collapse
Kissing me with your full hot lips
Both of us exhausted
Both of us pleased
Gratified and satisfied

Whisper in the dark

Blindfolded
Tied to the bed
Sense heightens
I smell your Polo Blue cologne
I hear you approaching me
Feel your breath caressing my skin
Cannot help but to moan
As you barely touch me
My body is on fire
Burning with desire
You feed me fruit
From your mouth to mine
Your kisses have always been sweet
Now they are even more delectable
Biting my bottom lip
As you draw circles on my neck
Hmmm
Bite me
You nibble softly
Moving across my body
With all the precision of a painter
Using his brush on a canvas
Sucking and licking my nipples
Biting each one
Hmmmm
shhhh
I love it rough
If I am not soaked something is wrong
Biting my stomach on the way down
Kissing my inner thigh
Dragging your nails along my legs
Driving me insane
Moaning your name
Feeling you blow on my clit
Right before sucking
All the wetness from my oasis
Sucking on my clit with each slurp

Hmmm yes suck my clit
Lick my split
Smelling my nectar
Hearing your tongue
Fight against the gusher
That has erupted between my thighs
Trying to grind your face but cannot
Hmmm
About to cum but you stop it
Coming up
Whispering in my ear
That I will only cum
When you want me to
Hmmmm
Damn stop torturing me
You go back to slowly drawing
What I imagine is your name around my clit
Hmmmm
Dammit I yell
Your tongue has me under your spell
You pick up speed
As you feed on my juices
Oh my gayness it feels so good
Then you stop
Whispering am I ready to cum
I quickly reply YES
You are sucking
Flicking
Licking
Slurping
Then before I knew it
I squirted
I feel it dripping
As I feel you sipping
I feel like ripping
The bedpost off the headboard
Moans quickly becomes screams
My heart is racing
You come up and kiss me
I smell the sweetness of my juices
Lingering on your lips

You go to remove my blindfold
Freeing me from my erotic darkness
As it is lifted up
I see you
It is at that moment
I cum again
You look so sexy soaked in my juices
Now lay down on top of me
Breast to breast
Pussy to pussy
Drifting off to sleep
Smiling to myself
As I whisper in your ear
Rest up now
It is your turn in the morning

Polo Boots

It feels good
To wake up to a kiss
Letting me know
That my presence is missed
Sleeping hard since last night tryst
Never knowing
Somebody could make me feel like this
So loved and desired
Being my motivation
Being the one to inspire me
Making me completely weak
Your head game
Left me speechless
The way you kept going
After I came
Left me breathless
My body losing control
Sad part is you know it
Sheets being ripped from the bed
All because you stayed on my head
Driving me insane
My legs shaking
Arching my back so much
Trying to run from your tongue lashing
It feels like I am going to break
After you have ate all you could
Drowning in what you could not
You got up
Went to clean your face
Thinking you was finished
Seeing you at the edge of the bed
Your strap attached
I could not help but to crawl to you
Sucking your strap
Though I know you cannot feel it
The visual stimulation
I give is sure to bring you to your knees

After you catch your nut
from my virtual head
You tell me to bend over
Put my face in the bed
Anticipation heightens
Feeling your mouth on my ass
You begin tossing my salad
Oh my gayness
here we go again
My legs losing feeling
While your tongue is doing the tornado spin
I was getting ready to cum again
You slide your strap in
Slowly taking your time
Feeding my pussy all 10 inches
I feel my fingers grabbing the sheets
I clench my teeth
Feeling the heat rushing over me
Slow and steady
You catch your rhythm
Feeling you touch my spots as you hit them
Going hard
Going deep
Feeling me drip all over the sheets
Dipping it low
Letting my pussy know
Who is in control
Now pounding it fast
As you slip your middle finger in my ass
Oh my gayness it is over now
I can take no more
I feel like the pounding you are giving me
We are going to fall through the bed onto the floor
Grabbing my shoulders
Pulling me back
Giving my ass a hard smack
At that moment I squirted all over you
My body forsaking me yet again
This time letting your strap win
Collapsing onto the bed
As you unstrapped your deadly weapon

Then I felt you sit on the bed
Looking back
It looked as if you were hanging your head
But quickly realizing
You were messing with your feet
I asked you what was wrong
You looked back and smiled at me
Saying nothing was wrong
Everything is right
Just trying to untie my polo boots
I think I tied them to tight
I turned over and laughed
And said that is what you get
Always trying to do new and extra shit
Right on cue
You replied
Not doing nothing new or extra
Just making sure that no matter what
At the end of it all
That you were pleased

Chronic Sex

I find myself
Undressing you with my eyes
Watching you as you cross your thighs
Such a lady in the streets
A straight freak when needed
In the car
On the stairs
In the club riding my strap in a chair
In the rain
In the snow
Leaving love marks
Letting people know
That you have been there
Underwear or no underwear
Nothing matters when I go down there
To your honey pot sticky and sweet
Getting it ready to take this meat
Always down for whatever
Does not matter the situation or weather
You are always willing to open to me
Even if I wanted to eat you in the car
Pulled to the side of the road
You do not care
If my face is buried down there
Tongue diving in deeply
Tongue lashing your clit quickly
Multitasking coming into play
As I suck your clit
Tongue fuck your hole
Taking your toy
To give you some ass play
You are humping my tongue
Riding those five inches like a boss
Every once in a while letting it slip down
Salad tossing you without hesitation
As I do that, you are grabbing my hair
Telling me not to stop

But of course I would not dare
Legs shaking
Back arching
Silence comes from your mouth
I continue to punish you down south
Trying to hold it in
Trying not to let me win
Then I suck your swollen clit
Between the gap in my teeth
Licking it quickly
You are screaming that you are about to skeet
Whether you squirt or skeet
I am drinking it all
Sucking you dry
Making sure none of your juices fall
Standing up
Licking my lips
Looking at you
Your dress pulled up above your hips
I know you label me hungry and greedy
I label you satisfied and happy
You ask me why that is
I smile and say
You look high as a kite
You sound as drunk as a skunk
I know without the shadow of doubt
That you will be sleeping like a baby tonight
The silence coming from you
Confirms that I am right
I am getting ready to take us home
I noticed that you were out like a light

Roadside Service

I arrived in town after a long bus ride
I see this handsome figure
Standing across the way smiling at me
I quickly walk up to her
Kissing her gently
Rubbing the back of her neck
Caressing her face in my hands
She grabs my bag with one hand
With the other hand grabs my hand
Escorting me to the car
Opening the door for me
I get in reach over and unlock her door
She gets in
Pulling off quickly
As she drives
I put my hand on her lap
Inches away from her pussy
The fact that I am caressing her thigh
Is turning her on so I moved my hand
So she could concentrate on her driving
I tried but I just cannot be good
I took her hand and suck her middle finger
Then proceeded to guide it under my dress
In between my thighs into my throbbing wet pussy
At first she was hesitant
Until she felt how hot and wet I was
She became more relaxed
Sliding her finger in and out my pussy
I open my legs wider
Giving her freedom
To plunge her fingers deeper into me
I feel myself losing control
Moans quickly becoming screams
I feel her swerving in and out of lanes
Speeding
Trying desperately to make it to her house
Before I explode all over the seat

At that very moment she pulls onto the shoulder
Shuts the car off
Get out walk to my side
Open the door
Helps me out
Telling Me to get in the backseat
As I do she quickly gets on her knees
Dives face first into my pussy
As she devours me
Hmmm
Eat your pussy
I know you are hungry
Now show me how much
You lick and suck my pussy
Like it was an over ripe peach
Hmmm yes
Eat it like you mean it
I feel my legs
Tightening around your head
You force my legs open
As I cum for you
You drink every drop completely
Not wasting anything
Afterwards you get up
Helping me back into the front seat
Only for you to join me
We proceed back to your house
Before we pull off
I tell you your turn will be coming soon
So when we walk through your door
Strip
Hit the floor
Get ready for fiyahead to work her magic

Quality Time

It is finally Friday
Time to spend with you
All week we have been busy with life
I am telling you now I will never be too tired
For you
To satisfy you
To please you
To release you
From your sexually frustrated cage
Free your rage upon me
I promise to take it all
Every scratch
That you brand my back with
Every bite
That you give me along my neck
Every lick
Upon my clit
Chills going through me
From the thought of you
Face buried between my legs
Making me beg
For you to devour this chocolate cream pie
Making me shake
Making my body go into spasms
Multiple orgasms being released
Flooding your face
Looking like a glazed donut
Feeling higher than high
I flip you over now it is your turn
Feeling the pleasure that runs through me
I kiss you soft and gentle
Caressing your nipples between my fingers
Moans escaping from your lips
Nibbling on your collarbone
Has you rubbing your legs together
With every action there is a reaction
Your wet aroma filling the air

As I slide down
Separating your legs
Licking your clit in circular motions
Flicking my tongue in and out your hole
Feeling your legs shaking
Tightening under the pressure
Sucking on your now swollen clit
Fat and juicy like a cherry
Your moans growing from a level 3
To a level 10 scream
As I feel you cum
Damn near smothering me
From your legs tightening around my neck
Sucking your juice from your box
I cannot stop
I will not stop
Until there is nothing left
Body finally relaxing
Toes still curled
Finally being released from your vice grip
Crawling up kissing you
My sweet smell mixed with yours
It is the most intoxicating smell
I have ever had the pleasure of making
Now curl up next to me
Lay your head on my chest
As I play in your hair
I start to think
Where did I put my underwear?
Wherever they are
They cannot be too far

Night at the Movies

Purse packed full of goodies
Tickets purchased
Rushing to see the previews
Found some good seats in the back
Me in a skirt
You in your dickies
Not knowing if we will really watch the movie
Whatever goes down I am ready
The show starts
I pull out the gummy worms
You pull out the skittles
I feel your hand on my thigh
I instantly exhale
Knowing that you will take me out my zone
Not even five minutes in
You have a fire raging from within
Wetness covering your hands
I watching you drop to your knees
The person on the screen is screaming
So am I
Except my scream is out of pleasure
As you stroke your tongue across my love button
I lose all sense of reality
Not caring who is around
Just concentrating on you going down
Pleasing me
Teasing me
Not concentrating on the movie
Just on us
As I come to a climax
You look around
Then quickly sit down
Thinking that we missed the movie
But it has only been five minutes
Since you had your face buried up in it
The lady on the screen has just been set free
Just like I was

The moment you decided
To show your favorite snack some love
On our night at the movies

Pussy Wine

Unlike most wine
This wine is best served warm
Straight from your pink satin box
Blacker the berry
Sweeter the juice
That runs from you
Gracing my lips
Making me take a sip
Intoxicating in every way
I cannot help but to suck you dry
While you are pulling your hair
Clawing the sheets
The CD I have playing has repeated
Not once but twice
I am lost in between your legs
Making you beg
You are losing thought of what is right or wrong
But still climaxing to my favorite song
The neighbors may know my name
While I am inventing sex
Let me overdose on you
As you ponder what is next
This love we are making is
Will be greater than sex

Catastrophic Orgasm

I will never brag on my head game
I rather show you what it is about
Phone conversations has your curiosity sparked
Sexy text of things you want me to do
Replies of me telling you what I need to do
To you to make you guess
Make you wet
Make you forget
About the bad day you had at work
Come over here to my lair
My dungeon
My sex palace
Once you are here you will never want to leave
Take your clothes off at the door
Follow the trail of rose petals
It will lead you to your sexual destiny
Close the door behind you
Once it is closed it will lock behind
Do not be afraid
Just lay back and enjoy
All your wildest dreams
Fantasies that are locked within
Shall be released tonight
Fantasies of honey being poured
All over your pedicured toes and sucked
Hmmm
You can hardly believe how good it is
Squeals escape you
Anticipation becomes you
Feeling my tongue
All over your feet
Sucking
Licking all stickiness from them
Once satisfied with the feelings I just provided
I proceed to your next fantasy of hot candle wax
Being dripped all over your caramel skin
I kiss you deeply before we begin

Looking into your eyes
I light the candle
Standing over your body
I trickle hot wax all over your nipples
You arch your back meeting each drip
Squeezing your legs together
You moan to drip some in your belly button
I quickly obliged you
I never knew how sexy red candle wax
Would look on your skin
I have completed this fantasy for you
There is one more left
So as I suck on your fingers
Tying each wrist to the headboard
Your ankles to the footboard
Leaving out of sight
Returning with all the ingredients
For one of my favorite desserts
Banana
Whip cream
Ice cream
Nuts
Sprinkles
Cherries
Hot fudge
Caramel
Your eyes becoming bigger
As you see what is on my tray
I lift your hips up
I place a plastic bag under you
Peeling the banana
Breaking it in half
Placing it in the folds of your pussy
Now putting two scoops of Vanilla ice cream
Shaking the can of whip cream
Strolling over to you
Telling you to open your mouth
As I spray whip cream your mouth
Quickly sitting my pussy on your face
I continue to make you my sundae
Even though your tongue has me shaking

But your distraction is no match for me
As I dive face first into my sexual dessert
Hmmm
Grinding on your face
As I cover mine in whip cream
Licking
Sucking
The drippings from your cream
The ice cream
Tasting so extra sweet
Satisfying the craving I had
Your tongue is being so invasive
Persuasive
As it finds my clit
Making my pussy spit
All over your face
Cumming so hard when you sucked my clit
Feeling hot
I get up
Kissing my juices off your lips
Now to finish the task I started
I crawl in between your legs
Eating the remainder of my dessert
Sucking and licking every drop of whip cream
Ice cream
Sprinkle
Nuts
Caramel and hot fudge
You are trying to run
It is too late
I told you
That you sealed your fate
When you closed the door
Hmmm
Damn
I do not know
I cannot stop eating you
Even though your pussy is almost clean
The taste of you is weighing on my senses
You have already had multiple orgasms
From my tongue attacking your pearl

Let me give you an eternal orgasm
Are you ready?
You barely moan yes
I undo your ankles
Bending your legs back
They meet your hands on the headboard
Folding you like a lawn chair
Shoving my tongue deep into your valley
Sucking and kissing your clit
Tossing your salad
Thoroughly and completely
Making your pussy squirt
Each time I dive in
Then it begins
The shaking of your legs
You are begging me not to stop
Not that I had any plans of stopping
Tongue fucking you until you bust
Your eyes rolling back in your head
Biting your lip
Trying not to scream
I lick and suck on your clit
The level 10 scream you released
Would have people thinking
I was killing you
They would be right
I am killing your pussy
Devouring your ass
Making your toes pop and curl
I feel your body start to relax
I release your legs from lock down
Untie your wrist
You embrace me and thank me with a kiss
Right before dozing off
Saying that you will sleep
As if you were taking an eternal slumber
I knew you would
After that catastrophic orgasm

Want to Join Me?

Laying in the bed alone
Waiting for you to come home
My mind still on last night
You had my mind gone
Body wide open
Sensitive to every touch
Heart racing
With each word that was spoken
I love the way
Your lips caress my ear
Kissing them gently
Pulling me near
Pulling my hair
Showing me that you are in charge
That rough shit
Turns me on
You know this
Why do you tease me so?
Exploring my body
Driving me crazy
Hmmm
The way you touch me
Got me on edge
Somewhere between
Pornographic reality and harsh fantasies
Is it possible that I have met my match?
Biting my lip
I doubt it
Even though my body is saying other wise
It is at that moment
I feel your hand between my thighs
Rubbing your finger across my clit
You are seeing how wet I can get
From your aggressiveness
Your kiss
The way you got me feeling
I cannot dismiss the lust

Passion and desire
Setting my inner being on fire
Rubbing
Kissing
Touching
Having me squirming
Re-learning my body
I never knew
Making love could feel so good
Now that I know
I do not want to go slow
I want to go fast
Letting my feelings out
My emotions taking over
While you tap this ass
Do not you stop
Until the sheets are off the bed
Do not stop until I am speechless
I do not want no words left to be said
Wanting to feel everything you have to offer
Show me that you know what to do
That it is yours
That you are here to claim it
Tame it
Own it
In return
I will give you my all
Every scratch mark
Love call
Bite mark
Bringing me to my climax
Making me drip all over your lips
Being prepared for what I am about to do
I am going on a trip to ecstasy
All I want to know is
DO YOU WANT TO JOIN ME?

Independent Intimacy

Coming in from dinner
I pop in a movie
Winding down before
You come over
Doing me
Like clockwork
You called
Cancelled
What is a girl to do
When she is out of batteries
She cannot depend on you
I turn the movie off
Went to my room
Lit some candles
It is time to make it do what it does
Took my clothes off
Laying across the bed
Imagining how it would be
If you were here
Giving me head
One hand on my nipple
Pinching it gently
Other hand on my clit
Rubbing it slowly
Biting my bottom lip
I took my finger away from my clit
Placing it into my mouth
Sucking on my fingertip
Making it wet
I continue to pet my fat kitty
The more I rubbed
The wetter I got
The hotter I got
No longer pinching my nipple
Instead rubbing it
Trying to keep my breathing steady
My pussy is sending Morse code

That it is ready
Throbbing
Jumping
Feeling the pulsating of my heart
From my constant rubbing
Inserting a finger to my flooded gate
Now I am rubbing my g-spot
That is the icing on the cake
Feeling me reach my destination
A thin line between paradise and ecstasy
Not stopping until my mission is complete
Raising my nipple to meet my tongue
A couple of flicks of my tongue
Over my hard nipple
I feel my pussy explode
Causing my body to ripple
Shake
Breathing heavily
Moaning your name
But you are not here
I keep going
Never slowing down
Never stopping
Until the intense feeling
Between my legs
Comes to a stop
Laying in the bed satisfied
Licking my lips
I turn over
Before going to sleep
I whisper your name
Sucking the cum off my fingertips
Thinking to myself
Damn
You missed out
On the ultimate sweet treat
But once again
You are not around
So I had to do me
Literally

Wedding Night

We have said our I do's
Sealed it with a kiss
We are on the way to our reception
Cuddled in the back of our limo
Embracing each other
Realizing that we are studsman and wife
That our blissful union is for life
It is at that moment
We stop moving
Wondering what is going on
You get out to question the driver
You came back looking disappointed
Saying we are stuck in traffic
Upset that we may miss the reception
You start to panic
Saying that we may miss our first dance
Cutting of the cake
All things traditional
I do not panic
I just look down at our wedding rings
Smiling
Thinking to myself
We may miss all that
But we took a major step
We gave ourselves to each other
We may miss the major events
The only thing that is on my mind
Is that tonight
Is our first time together
It has been a struggle
Keeping kisses from going any further
Since we are stuck in traffic
Who says we must wait?
I am your wife now
I am yours to take
Grabbing your face
Looking into your eyes

Telling you to calm down
Kissing you gently
Feeling your once tense body relax
Caressing my waist
Rubbing my back
You lift my dress
Revealing my white lace boy shorts
Without hesitation
You took them off
Feeling the heat rush from me
You kiss me deeply
Telling me that you love me
Your fingers start to roam
Finding my spot
You slide out of your seat
Remove your hand
Replacing it with your head
Cannot help but to gasp at first contact
Never experiencing anything like that
You take your time
Kissing my lips gently
Slowly twirling you tongue on it
Going in and out of it
Kissing my pussy
The way you kiss my lips
My eyes rolling to the back of my head
Aggressively biting my bottom lip
It feels so good
So intense
Never knowing you could make me feel like this
So open
So free
So hot
Ready to scream
Trying to close my legs
The feeling is unbearable
But you pick them up
Holding them open
Staying consistent
With the licks
Flicks and slurps

Stopping long enough
Telling me to fill you up
So you keep sucking on my clit
Clenching my teeth
Curling my toes
I feel my body get hot
Moaning do not stop
I came so hard
Squirting all over your tongue
Your lashes making me run
Lying down on the seat
Finishing your delicious creamy treat
Unzipping your pants
My pussy throbbing
Jumping
Pulsating
From the pleasure you just provided
You reveal a shiny chocolate strap
That you snuck into your duffle bag
So full of passion I pounce you
Taking it into my mouth
Sucking on it
Deep throating it
Making it slippery and wet
Before slowly inserting you into me
I moan under the pressure
Riding it slow at first
Getting use to your 10-inch strap
Hmmmm
Damn
It feels so good
Looking down as you bite your lip
Grabbing my hips
Bouncing me up and down on your strap
It is turning me on
Hearing our skin slap against each other
You flip me onto my back
Going deeper into me
Kissing me passionately
Feeling your energy
Combined with mine

Scratching your back
The deeper you go
The more I suck your bottom lip
You are moaning
I am screaming
Our bodies shaking
Us kissing each other
Finally feeling the limo start to move
We get dressed
Put our shoes on
With minutes to spare
We made it to our reception
As we had our first dance
I asked you
Babe do you have my underwear?
Looking into my eyes
Kissing me on the forehead
You winked saying what do you think?

White Out

Always going to the beach
We decided to try something new
We rented out a cabin with a beautiful view
Not crazy about cold weather
Since I am with you it does not matter
If you promise to keep me warm
So, my teeth will not chatter
I decided to take a shower
While you get the fireplace going
I am finishing up
Jump out the shower
Opening the door
I see you standing there holding flowers
Vanilla scented candles quickly filling the air
You take a towel
Wrap it around my hair
Took me by my hand
Lead me to a pulled out chair
Sitting down you gently unwrap my hair
I wonder what you are about to do
Hearing you plug in the blow dryer
Grabbing my favorite brush
Brushing through my hair
As the heat blows through my hair
I feel so turned on you just do not know
How wet I have gotten
Just from this simple act of kindness
The hair on my head now dry
But down below is soak and wet
You present me with dinner
But I want dessert
You to be specific
Laid on this table
In front of me spread eagle
But I am going to be patient
I am waiting on you
I know you have a lot of cleaning to do

As you do that I drop my robe
Jumping on the counter
Eating the chocolate dipped strawberries
That you had prepared for dessert
Walking over running your fingers up my thighs
Cupping my ass in your hands
Picking up a strawberry
Holding it between my teeth
You bite the tip off
Then proceed to kiss me
Hmmm
The intensity growing between us
Anticipation grows with each caress
Picking me up
Putting me on the glass table
Disappearing for a moment
Returning with the cream cheese
Spreading it all over me
Not missing a spot
Your touch is making me hot
Laying here covered in sticky sweet goodness
I want you to ravage me
I do not expect nothing less
One lick of my nipple
The cream cheese disappeared
You eat it off me
Like you were scared it might melt
Before you could eat it all
Your aggressiveness is making me wetter
The way you work your way down
To my cream cheese covered pussy
Licking it hard to make sure nothings left
Then slurping it into your mouth
I feel my insides quiver
The fact that you are working my pussy
Like its no tomorrow
Grabbing the back of your head
Spreading my legs
Shoving you deeper
Feeling your tongue entering me
All I hear echoing in the room is my wetness

The more you suck on my lips and clit
The more I cum
Repeatedly
You reach up to play with my nipples
Instead I suck your middle finger into my mouth
Moaning from the pressure of the suction from my lips
I am moaning from the licking from yours
Before I realize it, you are shaking
I am shaking and squirming
We are both Cumming
Neither one of us tapping out
Steadily going until there is nothing left
Then just like clockwork
We both retreat into ourselves
You passed out face first on my pussy
Me passing out
Sprung across the table
Us trying to gather ourselves
To proceed into the bedroom
Once we made it there
Collapsing across the bed
Cuddling up close to me
I guess our plans are cancelled for tomorrow
Asking why that was
You pointed towards the window
Which was covered in snow
Saying how are we supposed to get through all that

Whips and Chains

It is the weekend
Time for the fun and games to begin
I wore a black and red leather cat suit
You wore spiked black leather dog collar
Tonight, you shall be my slave
Because you have been very naughty
I am going to spank you until you behave
But first things first
Get on your knees
Crawl over to me
Yes
Slow and steady just like that
Like I am your prey
You are the jungle cat
Now stand up
Let me put your leash on you
Everything that is about to happen
I am sure is going to turn you on
Now follow me over to this wall
I am about to chain you up
I do not want you to fall
Pleasure and pain will put you in your place
You have been acting up
Thinking I would forget
I was just taking notes
Using it as an outlet
So, relax as I put this ball gag in
I pick up your favorite paddle
Swinging it against the wind
Your anticipation is growing
I can tell by your breathing
With a stern voice I ask
After tonight what are you going to do?
But nothing but silence came from you
I leaned back
Swinging coming full force
Giving your ass I nice hard smack
You did not flinch

Letting out I sigh
I had to give something else a try
I went to the drawer
Pulled out my whip
It was at that moment
I saw sweat starting to drip
Down your face
Onto the floor
Breath that was once heavy
I cannot hear no more
I repeat the question again
A lot softer and more feminine
After tonight what are you going to do?
But nothing but silence came from you
With the flick of my wrist
I swung my whip
Grazing it across your back
Saying if you do not answer now
I am going to bring out the candle wax
So, like the naughty girl you are
You said nothing
I had the pleasant task of turning you around
Leading you to this reclining table
Handcuffing you securely to it
Making sure that everything was stable
Grabbing one of the lit red candles
Walking back over to you
Seeing you try to brace yourself
Before I even start dripping candle wax on you
I ask you one last time
After tonight what are you going to do?
Again, nothing but silence came from you
So, I had to do what I had to do
Tilting my hand
Letting the wax drip onto your skin
That is when the moaning began
Each drip of the hot wax
Made the volume of your moans intensify
Opening the drawer
Pulling out your next source of torture
Vibrating nipple clamps

I knew was going to send you over the edge
Before attaching them
I hear you trying to beg
It is too late for you
You had your chance
To act right
To obey
Lay back
Relax and take what is coming to you
I proceed to drip wax all over you
Hearing your moans become whimpers
I take the ball gag out
I want to hear the words
Coming out of your mouth
Placing the candle stick back on the shelf
Grabbing our new glass toy
Sucking on it
Making it as wet as I could
Before continuing
I spread your legs
Strapped your ankles into the harness
I do not need you moving for nothing
Once I was done
I licked your already swollen clit
You taste so sweet
With every lick from my tongue
I see you curling up your feet
Trying to hold onto what is left of your sanity
Sucking on your clit
I take your glass dick
Sliding it in slowly inch by inch
I feel your thighs shaking under the
From having triple the pleasure
Your whimpers
Speeding towards screams
Your glass dick covered in your cream
Shoving it faster and deeper
Turning and twisting it
Hitting your g-spot
Repeatedly and constantly
Squirming

Moaning
Whining
Whimpering and screaming
Saying that you are about to cum
But before you do
I asked
After tonight what are you going to do?
You scream as you came
Always be ready and prepared to serve you

Birthday Sex

Glad to see another year
Waking up to you is even better
Smelling your scent
Still fresh on my lips
Sweet and sticky
A gift that keeps on giving
Making my birthday better
Unwrapping you
Like a gift unexpected
Allowing me to play with you
In ways we only talked about
Not used to being submissive
Thanks for submitting
You are about to experience
Unimaginable pleasure
Kissing a trail from your pedicured toes
Up to your knees
Biting the space behind them
Continuing my journey uptown
To your thick thighs
Licking
Sucking
Biting on your tattoos
On the way up
The smell of your wetness
Seeping out
There's still more ground to cover
Gliding my tongue
Over your belly button
Making my way up
Nipples harden
Making eye contact with you
Giving them the royal treatment
Kissing on your neck
Panting and breathing through each kiss
Releasing your full lips
From the suction of my lips
It is time to eat

I have been anticipating this all day
Pussy sitting pretty
Like a slice of red velvet cake
Taking my time
Savoring the taste
Giving my tongue permission
Making love to your pussy
The slower I go
The more you shake and jerk
Squirting
Locking your legs around my head
Not stopping
Cleaning up my mess
Lying there
Trying to catch your breath
Licking my lips
Relishing the fact
This was the best birthday sex
I have ever had

Fun Size is the Right Size

5'5 packed with the dominance I crave
Taking me on this intimate journey
Commanding submission
I am not use to
Bedroom eyes
Putting me in a trance
Her smile makes the sun jealous
Her touch makes my flood gates open up
Caressing me
Making me cum
From the inside out
Putting in overtime
With her there is no sleep
No creeping
Only penetration
Gliding slowly into my pool of love juices
Anticipating her kiss
Mixing two worlds
Love and lust
Making love to my mind
Preparing my body to be fucked several ways
Starting at my toes
Kissing and sucking each one
Prowling my body like we are in the wild
Running her fingers and lips over my hot skin
Temperature rising with each touch
Teasing me
Blowing on my clit
Passing it
Paying attention to my breast
Damn
You have them hard
Waiting to invade your mouth
Sucking
Biting
Making me squirm
Hunger in your eyes
Fire between my thighs

Kissing me
It will be all over
Sucking my bottom lip
Kissing and stroking simultaneously on my clit
Setting my body a blaze
Removing your lips from mine
Putting your finger in my mouth
Sucking it clean
Moving down
Towards your favorite thing to eat
Kissing it gently
Damn
I know I am in trouble
Savoring the taste
Losing myself
Losing my soul to you
Starting off slow
Losing yourself between my legs
Begging for completion
Not yet
Just relax
Rubbing on my g-spot
Sucking my clit
Stopping long enough
Telling me to look at you
Feeling us unite
Giving me permission to cum
Climbing the scales of pleasure
Looking at you
As I cum
Latching onto me
Not missing the opportunity
Showing the love you have for me
Feeling that and so much more
Multiple orgasmic waves
Still looking into your eyes
You have me so open
But I do not mind
Fun size
You are the perfect size
That will always be the perfect size for me

About the Author

       Raven the Serial Poet known as Makala Taylor has been a writing poetry since the age of 13. It all started with her love of Edgar Allen Poe. After experiencing a tragic event she used poetry as verbal therapy. In doing so she discovered her love for verbal expression. Who knew the simple expressions of a young girl would turn into mental stimulation.

       Raven continues to make progress in her passion for writing, her enthusiasm for raising eyebrows and creating shock factors with her play on words. Which she displays with her latest book "Enter into My Dungeon" a book that taps into the darker side of erotic poetry. Not stopping at poetry, she has a Podcast called "Raven Rants" where she sparks up conversation about topics that many can but will not talk about. She also is working on her business Queen Pettilicious Apparel which will sell everything from Novelty T-shirt to Wrist Bands with a cause. Raven the Serial Poet is making waves, but the question is are you ready for what will come next.